The Child's World of
JOY

Library of Congress Cataloging in Publication Data

Moncure, Jane Belk.
Joy / Jane Belk Moncure
   p.   cm.
Originally published: c1982.
Summary: Simple text and scenes depict such joys as the first
snowman of the year, hot cocoa, flying a kite, holding a baby
sister for the first time, and being hugged by Mom and Dad after
they've been away on a trip.
ISBN 1-56766-299-4 (hardcover)
1. Joy in children—Juvenile literature.   [1. Joy.]
I. Title.
BF723.J6M66   1996
179'.9—dc20
                              96-11863[B]
                              CIP
                              AC

The Child's World of
JOY

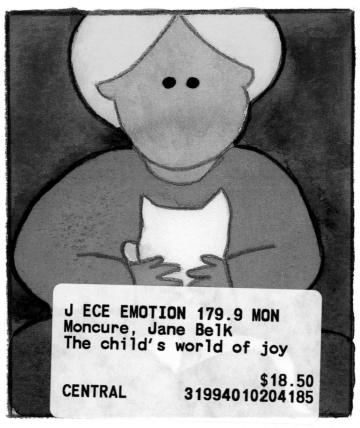

By Jane Belk Moncure • Illustrated by Mechelle Ann

THE CHILD'S WORLD

What is joy?

Joy is a happy feeling inside that bubbles out in a smile when your best friend comes to play.

Making the first snowman of the year—that's joy! And after you have been out in the snow, joy is a cup of hot cocoa with a marshmallow on top.

Joy is playing the drum in a rhythm band.

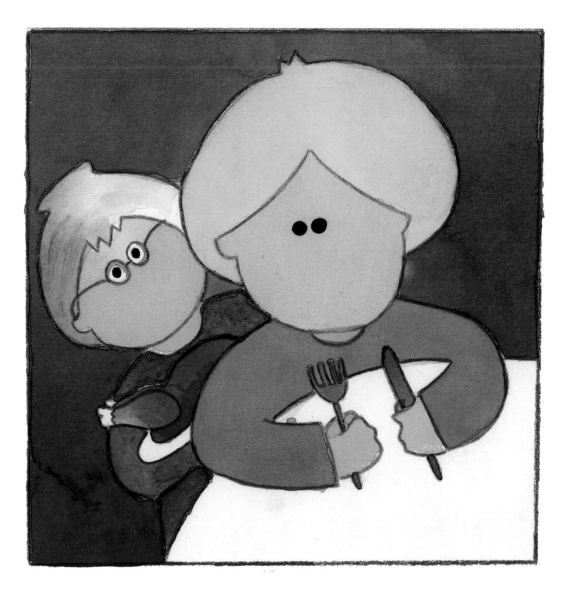

And joy is Thanksgiving dinner at Grandma's house.

When you go to a new school, where you don't think you'll have any friends, and then you see a boy you know—that's joy!

Joy is running barefoot on the beach with the sand tickling your toes.

Joy is finding your kitten after she's been lost for two days.

And joy is making a kite that flies—and doesn't crash.

When you go to the zoo and walk a long way to see the giraffes and the zebras and the monkeys, and then you see a water fountain—that's joy!

Joy is when the kids are choosing teams and your brother chooses you to be on his side, even though you're the smallest.

And joy is when you hold your baby sister for the first time and she goes to sleep in your arms.

When it's hot and you've worked hard to put up the tent, joy is hearing Dad say, "Let's go swimming."